PIZZA for BREAKFAST

Written and illustrated by
Maryann Kovalski

KIDS CAN PRESS LTD.
Toronto

To Steven Jack

Kids Can Press Ltd. acknowledges with
appreciation the assistance of the Canada
Council and the Ontario Arts Council in
the production of this book.

Canadian Cataloguing in Publication Data

Kovalski, Maryann
    [Frank and Zelda]
    Pizza for breakfast

Originally published as: Frank and Zelda.
ISBN 1-55074-152-7

I. Title. II. Title: Frank and Zelda.

PS8571.093P59   1995   jC813'.54
C94-932263-6
PZ7. K79Fr   1995

Text and illustrations copyright © 1990 by
Maryann Kovalski

Kids Can Press Ltd.
29 Birch Avenue
Toronto, Ontario, Canada
M4V 1E2

Book design by Maryann Kovalski
Printed and bound in Hong Kong

PA 95 0 9 8 7 6 5 4 3 2 1

Frank and Zelda owned a small pizza shop next to Mel's Summer Hat and Glove Factory. Business wasn't just good—it was booming.

The workers at the factory came for lunch. The shopkeepers came for dinner. Frank made the pizza and Zelda served the customers.

It was a lot of work but they were happy, even though they didn't know it at the time. Frank complained the kitchen was too hot and the work never stopped. Zelda said her feet hurt from all the running.

Late at night, Zelda would gaze at the factory and think, "Someday people will get fed up with hats and gloves in the summer. We should make a plan, Frank and I."

But they never made a plan. They'd clean up, go to bed and face another busy day.

Zelda was right. The day did come when people tired of wearing hats and gloves in the summer. The factory closed. The workers moved away. Nobody came to the restaurant anymore.

The days were long and sometimes Frank and Zelda quarrelled. When Zelda talked, Frank didn't listen. So Zelda talked less and less. They passed the time silently, wishing for the old days.

One day, a man appeared.

"Excuse me," he said. "Might I see a menu?"

"A menu?" asked Zelda.

"Zelda, a menu! The man wants a menu! He is a customer and he wants a menu!"

Frank ran to the kitchen. Zelda took the man's hat, dusted it off and poured him a glass of water.

Frank concocted the biggest, the juiciest, the all-round best pizza he had ever made. He lined the edge with pepperoni and made circles of olives and anchovies.

The man ate heartily and complimented Frank and Zelda on their fine pizza and excellent service. He was at the door when Frank found his voice. "Wait! You forgot to pay!"

"Oh," said the man, "I haven't any money. I never carry money. Just kindness and good will."

"Call the police," said Zelda.

The man became tearful and begged, "Please don't. I'll give you anything you wish. Really. Go on, make a wish."

"Ha!" said Frank and Zelda together, for neither believed in magic.

"I wish I had a paying customer," said Frank. "No, make it a thousand—every day and forever."

At that moment, a busload of basketball players stopped in front of the restaurant. Frank and Zelda were amazed and turned to the little man.

But he was gone.

After the basketball players, more people came. It was dawn when the last customer left and the place was clean. Arm in arm, Frank and Zelda went up to their apartment, tired and grinning.

"Just like the old days, eh, Frank?" laughed Zelda.

"Even better," Frank answered as he squeezed Zelda's shoulder.

They were deep in dreams when they were awakened by banging downstairs.

"What do you want?" Frank called to the gathered crowd.

"Pizza!" the people cheered. Frank and Zelda were astonished.

"But it's morning," said Frank. "You don't want pizza for breakfast!"

"Pizza for breakfast! Pizza for breakfast!"

As the crowd chanted, Frank and Zelda dressed and rushed downstairs.

They were so tired
they got the orders mixed up.
And *still* the customers kept
coming. During the worst of it,
Zelda spotted the little man again.

"Wonderful, isn't it, Zel?" he said.

"HELP!" cried Zelda. "I wish I had some help around here!"

That night they didn't clean up. They just fell into bed and
went straight to sleep.

The next morning, there was a gentle tap tap tapping at the front door. Afraid of what might be down there, they peeked out from behind tightly drawn curtains. Frank ripped open the curtains and cried, "Look Zelda! Waiters!" Hundreds of smiling waiters formed a neat line.

It worked out well at first, but as the restaurant filled, all those waiters bumped into one another. Frank and Zelda didn't quite know what to do. From under a table popped the smiling face of the little man.

"I never forget a good deed or a good pizza," he said.

"I don't know if I believe in magic, but I sure wish we had a bigger restaurant," said Zelda.

The man grinned and lowered the tablecloth.

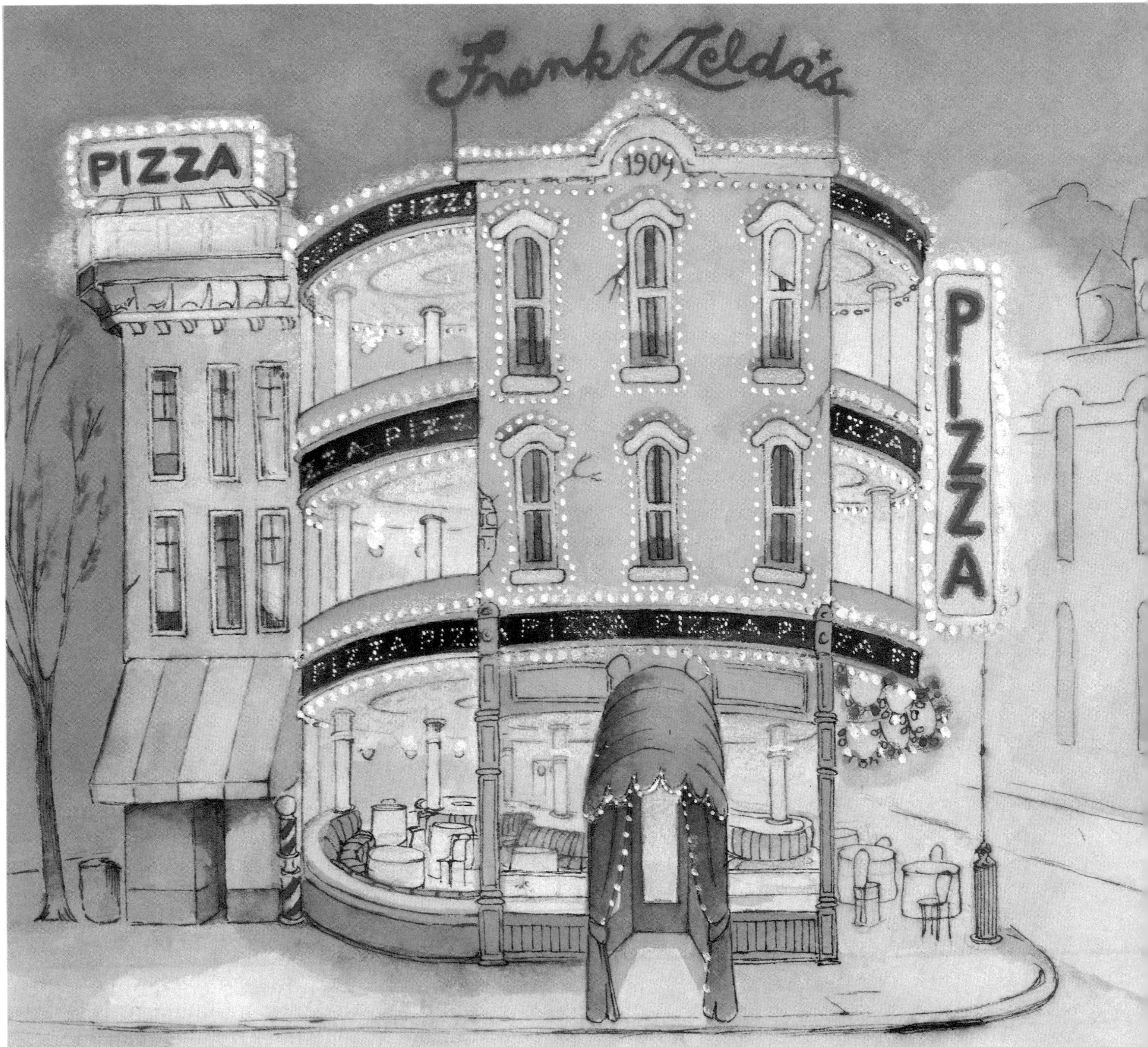
Frank & Zelda's
PIZZA
1909
PIZZA

Frank and Zelda couldn't sleep that night. They stared at the ceiling imagining what would greet them in the morning.

At dawn, they rushed down to the street and gaped at their new restaurant.

Night and day, day and night, the business never slowed. It seemed all the world wanted to eat at Frank and Zelda's, and all Frank and Zelda wanted to do was feed them.

But after a while, Zelda's feet ached. The kitchen
was hotter than ever. The waiters grew tired and grumpy.

One night, a badly behaved group of customers threw food.
Soon the whole place was brawling. Zelda tried to stop them, but
things were out of hand. She ran to the kitchen and into Frank's
arms.

They held each other tight. The doors swung open and in slid the little man.

He looked sadly at Frank and Zelda. "I feel a bit responsible for all this," he said.

"I wish we'd never got those lousy wishes!" moaned Frank.

Immediately, all was silent outside. Frank and Zelda inched their way towards the doors and opened them a crack. They stuck their heads out. There was nobody there. It was as if none of it had happened.

Frank locked the door. Zelda made a pot of tea.

"You know what, Frank," she said. "I think it's time we made a plan."

"I think you're right," said Frank.

They sipped their tea and made their plan.

Soon, Frank and Zelda were happy again.

And this time, they knew it.